A MONK'S TALE

By

Matthew B. Berg

Woodfall Press
P.O. Box #6011
Holliston, MA 01746

eBook ISBN: 0-9785791-4-3
Paperback ISBN: 979-8-60-082817-9

Printed in the United States of America
10 9 8 7 6 5 4 3 2 1

STEAL THIS BOOK!

Well, you don't even have to steal it! You can get an electronic copy of it for FREE!

Claim your copy here:

https://matthewbberg.com

Join the Crafter's Guild!

Become a member and become part of the story.

- Members of the guild are always the first to hear about Matthew's new books and publications.
- Members will receive access to free behind-the-scenes content, such as maps, character sheets, and other Crafter artifacts—as we create them.
- Finally, some lucky guild members will have the opportunity to become beta readers for book two (and beyond!).

Check out the back of the book for information on how to become a guild member.

To my readers.

MAP OF KNOWN LANDS

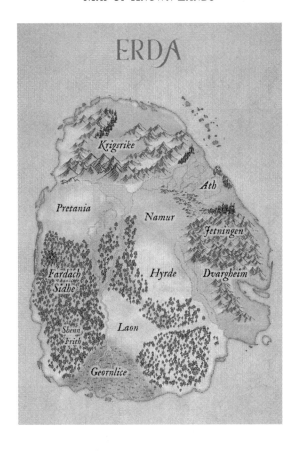

PROLOGUE

Cedric looked around the mostly empty room. Almost everything had been carefully bundled up in crates. He'd let his aide take charge of most of the items in his study—predominantly books, scrolls, and other loose writings. But he'd asked him to leave the packing of his trophy shelf to him. He couldn't bear the thought that those items might get damaged or lost, so he would see to them personally.

The shelf was more cluttered than he liked. But the items it contained were ones with which he would have a hard time parting.

A troll's tooth. A bit gruesome, but there could be no better reminder of what he had undergone.

A smooth grey adder stone on a simple twine lanyard.

A delicate wand of wenge wood. The elf who'd passed it on to Cedric claimed it had been a gift from the tree itself.

A raw chunk of silver ore from the dwarven king.

A fearsome talon he had found in the mountains of Ath. The Krigares were convinced it was a dragon's claw, though, strangely, it seemed to be made of stone.

And of course, there were his journals. He'd started writing them when he was campaigning with the king so many years ago. And for the most part, he'd done a fair job of keeping up with the habit.

He grabbed an empty crate and set it at his feet. And then he plucked his oldest journal from the shelf. It was smaller than the others. More weathered and tatty. He brought the journal up to his nose and inhaled. The earthy smells of leather, ink, and vellum relaxed him. And he leaned back in his chair and stared idly out the window. Dawn would be breaking soon.

He raised the book to his nose a second time and took an even deeper breath. Still calming and familiar, though not quite as transporting as the first whiff. On a whim, he uncoiled the leather cord that held the pages together from around the button on the journal's cover. And he flipped to the first entry.

TROLL PATROL

J*ournal of Cedric Warke, Year 850*
Ath/Krigsrike—Day 280

The king *himself told me I should keep a journal. Well, he told a handful of us at once. But that's the same thing to me. He said that officers were under an obligation to document their activities for posterity. I don't know about all that. But when the men are carousing around their fires with meat and mead, and the five of us knights are scratching away at our diaries like a bunch of scribes, it's hard to think ahead to a day when anyone would care about what we're doing up here.*

Anyway, I suppose I should write about our mission, and the things we've encountered. That's the interesting stuff, I'd say.

Our mission is killing trolls. Vile, filthy creatures, they are. So far, we've skimmed along between the edge of Namur and Krigsrike. And we went as far as Pretania to the west. The Krigares keep the troll numbers down near their own cities. So we only encountered pockets of them along the way. And the locals usually steered us where we needed to go to find them. We've also been to Dvargheim and Ath—to maintain good relations with the dwarves and giants. I hope the dwarves especially appreciate our efforts. We lost some good men in Dvargheim. And, may the gods save us, we even took a run at the beasts in their own home in Jetningen. Didn't think we were going to make it out of there. I couldn't believe their numbers.

WE SAILED AS FAR as the northern reach of Ath, and we've been harvesting spars from the trees at the edge of the Krigsrike. We're technically on Krigare land right now—with the blessing of the local Krigare "king." And our king was nearly overtaken by a pack of trolls this morning.

The foul beasts came pouring out of the forest like a black wave. I remember the smell most of all. Of sweat and rot and worse. And then they were upon us. The king didn't even have time to draw his sword before one latched on to his arm.

The scales saved him. And I nearly cut the monster in half while it tried to worry its teeth through his metal sleeve. Fortunately for us, the wave was over in moments. A dozen of the coarse and twisted things lay in the snow.

And I suppose I should mention that I took a bite below the knee on the back of my left leg. I was walking through the carnage after the fight, and one of the things that I'd sworn was dead a moment before came to life and sank its foul jaws into me. It was a quick enough thing to kill it. And we all agreed afterward that it made sense to make a pile of their carcasses and burn the rest of them. But I'll be damned if my leg doesn't still ache like a bad tooth all these hours later. One of the sergeants has me drinking some Krigare potion he made from brandy and one of the local plants. And he put a plaster of the stuff on the bite too. He said it's going to get worse before it gets better.

ATH—DAY 310

THIRTY DAYS! It's been thirty cursed days since my last entry in this notebook. I'm finally strong enough to hold a quill again today. My leg healed badly—and slowly. The Krigares say the trolls' spit is poison. The sergeant said it's not so much poison as rotten. And the rot gets into you when they bite you—or even claw you sometimes.

About a week ago, I regained my wits from the fog of the disease, and I apologized to the king and my men. The king was gracious—it probably helped that I'd seen him through his own pinch that day. And truth be told, I think the men were grateful for the break. But the nights are getting colder. And the sea is freezing up. So I'm sure they'll tire of what passes for fun among the Krigares long before spring.

CEDRIC GENTLY CLOSED the book and placed it deliberately on the desk before him. Who was that innocent young knight?

He rarely looked back through his journals these days. When he had been younger, he would read through them frequently. To remind himself what he'd been doing. And perhaps to convince himself that his actions were sound. He knew well now how time and distance could help to provide perspective on one's decisions. Even today, in skimming over his diaries, he expected to observe things that would give him pause and cause him to consider how he might handle something differently if he were given a chance to live the moment again.

With a renewed sense of purpose, he picked up his journal again and flipped to the middle.

2

ADJUTANT

J ournal of Cedric Warke, Year 858
  Arlon—Day 110

THERE'S SOMETHING AFOOT. *But I haven't yet fig-
ured out what it is. As adjutant to the knight-captain, I'm in a strange position. Some men treat me
as though I am the knight-captain himself. And
others don't even notice I'm there. The former are
harder to read. I see suspicion among them where
there may be none. And more often than not, I'll
get nothing more than a few paltry words in re-
sponse when I'm looking for answers. But the
latter are much more useful. I cultivate my rela-
tionships with such men. Because I know how
useful they are.*

*Allerton is one such. He's a young knight
from the Hyrden border with Laon. And he's*

quick to chatter on about everything and anything. From news back home to the latest gossip from the barracks. He said something the other day that stuck with me. He mentioned a muster of knights, and how he'd been unable to attend. I'm not sure the significance of what he said even occurred to him. But I was careful not to dig too deeply too quickly. I tried to ask him about it as casually as I could.

CEDRIC REMEMBERED THAT CONVERSATION. It had been but a tiny moment in a much larger tapestry of conflict between Hyrde and Laon. And when he'd picked at the thread, he'd discovered that a handful of Laonese knights were in the early stages of a rebellion.

Associates of the mutineers had later made an attempt on Cedric's life for informing the king. And concerned Cedric would be an easy target with his bad leg, the king had decided it best to send him away. That was what brought him back to the Krigsrike.

How was it that he could remember that conversation with Allerton so clearly all these years later, and yet other memories stayed with him only with the foggiest detail?

He flipped ahead.

3

KRIGSRIKE

J ournal of Cedric Warke, Year 865
    Krigsrike—Day 183

I'VE DONE my time up here and made a fair reck-
oning of myself. My presence has allowed me to
disarm a handful of disputes that would have
flamed up if they had relied on letters to Arlon
and back. But my mind is getting as soft as my
troll-weakened body. So I've put in for a transfer
to Ekszer Hegy, where the king has graciously
allowed me to receive an extended education.

Which isn't to say my time among the Krigare hasn't had its moments. Just yesterday was
the Midsummer Festival. If every day were as
long as yesterday, I fear I'd drink too much and
get far too little sleep. But to celebrate with aban-
don, as these folks do once a year, is understand-

able when you've lived through seven years of cold and dark winters, as I have.

There is a woman here, a widow, who lost her husband to the sea many years back. As I made my way door to door so ponderously last night, I planned my route to end at hers. She fed me, as she'd fed the other villagers who'd come round before me. But when her last visitor had gone, I spent the night and warmed her bed as well. I'm not sure either of us is looking for more than what we had last night. But I'm also sure it did us both a world of good. I will miss the Krigare ways. They lack a certain refinement in manners and culture. Their food is often simple. And their art is sometimes crude. But they make up for it all through an exuberance of spirit.

HE TURNED to the end of the first journal and sought out his final entry.

4

EKSZER HEGY

Journal of Cedric Warke, Year 867
  Dvargheim/Ekszer Hegy—Day 200

I'VE BEEN HERE NEARLY *a month, and I've been so
preoccupied I've forgotten to keep up with my
journal! But the distractions at this citadel aren't
your typical ones—wine and women. Mostly it's
the books they have in this place. Every class-
room, bedroom, and lecture hall has dozens—or
more.*

*Most of the scholars on the island are
studying magic. Only a handful are here for more
traditional educations. But those of us who aren't
interested in practicing magic are left well alone
—which only makes our studying that much easier. Even among the Krigares, I never knew such
peace and quiet as they have here at Ekszer Hegy.*

I'm far younger than all the other traditional students. But I'm of an age with a few of the apprentice mages. We have taken to socializing once a week—during weekend prayers. I can tell that Deoddyn isn't quite at ease with the whole thing. Like many here, he isn't overly comfortable with people. And perhaps he is more pious than he admits. But Ydenia seems to revel in it. She is a bit of a firebrand, I'm afraid. She tells me herself how she torments her teachers. And I can tell by watching Deoddyn's face that she isn't exaggerating. But there's also something contagious about her energy. I fear that she could become a distraction for me if I'm not careful.

CEDRIC SHOOK HIS HEAD. His first journal ended there. And reading that particular entry was a bit like picking at a scab. But once he'd unwound the cord from the book and cracked its pages, he'd known that it was inevitable he'd allow himself the self-indulgence to remember . . .

5
_____

YDENIA

Cedric looked over at the woman riding the chestnut palfrey beside him. Ydenia was beautiful. Not just to him. She was really beautiful. He could tell it wasn't just a spell she'd cast over him in particular. He could see the way people acted around her. Both men and women treated her as someone special. But when he told her as much, she would deny it. There had been mornings, when her breath was a bit ripe, her eyes were baggy, and his own head was cloudy from too much drink the night before, when he would question himself. Was it an illusion? Did the drink affect his judgment? Could she truly have cast a spell on him? Was that possible?

But then they would both take hot baths and eat some breakfast, and the doubts would fade again.

He looked over his shoulder, back down the forest path. The spruces were straight and so very tall he had to crane his neck to see the canopy. They lost their lower branches as they grew, so the trunks gave the impression of columns. And the forest had the feel of a living cathedral. He expected to see goshawks and owls flashing their wings in the branches above. He knew that, while rarely seen, it was true enough they were here aplenty.

Yet these trees were saplings compared to those that made up the city they had just left. Aoilfhionn. A place you could be told about, but you could never appreciate its transporting majesty until you walked among those ancient and beautiful trees yourself.

Despite Aoilfhionn's beauty, they were on their way to Shenn Frith now.

Ydenia had been convinced that the elf mages could teach her things she couldn't learn from the wizards at Ekszer Hegy. And since Cedric had never been there himself, he'd asked for, and been granted, permission to travel to the elven homeland to continue his studies. As always, he was sure the king hoped for missives letting him know what the elves were up to. For Cedric's purposes, there were said to be ancient scrolls in Aoilfhionn concerning the gods. He hoped they could answer some of the questions he had about the gods' origins.

But Ydenia . . . did not make herself overly welcome there. And after weeks of attempting to engage the elderly elven scholars in his research, Cedric had to confess he hadn't felt much affection from the elves himself.

"Some of those elves were hundreds of years old." She dispelled his musings with a statement that bore the conviction of someone who had been mulling over a calculation for a long time. "Based on the people they claim to have known, and the events in which they participated, I estimate the oldest might have lived close to seven hundred years."

Cedric decided to goad her a bit for disrupting his reverie. "They are nearly gods, then."

She squinted her eyes and glared at him, as if she knew he was looking to draw a reaction from her. "You and your theories! I'm telling you, I don't care whether the gods are truly *gods* or not! If they can live forever, then they are gods as far as I'm concerned!"

Cedric smiled, happy she'd taken the bait. He loved the banter of a good debate. It was probably the thing he missed most about leaving Ekszer Hegy, having access to other scholars to argue about philosophy, science, and religion.

He continued. "Being immortal doesn't make them *gods*! Besides, I'm not even sure they are truly immortal. Not in the way you mean."

Ydenia responded quickly. "Don't start with your 'point in time' argument again! I don't care if they were present on the day that everything began. If the gods can live forever, and . . . frankly, this might even be supported by your theory that they aren't truly gods, then why can't we?"

Cedric smiled again, and he let her question go unanswered for a moment. She had an infatuation with mortality, or rather, extending one's life.

After her fifth year at Ekszer Hegy, she'd been named a journeyman magician. To hear her tell it, she'd never go higher than that with the current head wizard in place. As soon as she'd ceased to be an apprentice, with its rigid curriculum of courses carefully spread across the spectrum of magical studies, she had been granted the right to study independently.

While her education up to that point had ensured she understood the basic tenets of magic within each "school," tradition held that she could now devote her efforts toward whichever school of magic suited her abilities and desires. But Cedric knew there was really no school that focused on longevity. The closest was probably healing. Hence her desire to study with the elf mages, who were the only magic users who currently practiced healing. Ydenia had said something about how the last recorded human to have practiced healing magic had died centuries earlier, and worse, he'd had an unwholesome reputation for experimentation that had sullied the entire branch of study.

But unfortunately, the elves didn't approve of Ydenia. While he'd not been present for her falling-out, he guessed that her impatience, or possibly her imperiousness, had been her undoing. She didn't like being put off. She didn't like hearing no. And she wasn't prepared to study with the elf mages for fifty years to gain the knowledge she sought.

And so they were on their way to Shenn Frith to seek out their famed shamans, who practiced spirit magic, and who Ydenia knew had always been given free access to the knowledge and teachings of the elven mages.

Cedric's smile became a smirk. And he half-heartedly launched one last barb. "I am rather more worried about the old gods' morality than their longevity. They seem more concerned about themselves than about any higher purpose. Usen's One God, on the other hand, is said to have created everything you see here—all for us!"

Ydenia picked up her pace and came alongside him. "Nobody's ever seen your *One God* before, have they? How do you even know *He* exists?" She spurred her horse on again and pulled ahead of him.

His smile soured. *Oh well. So much for good-natured banter!* He never knew when she was going to humor him and his explorations of thought, and when she was going to lose patience with him. He gently tapped his heels against his horse's flank to catch up.

6

FEATHERS, FURS, AND BONES

The shamans of Shenn Frith disturbed Cedric. Their feathers, furs, and bones. Their smoking bowls of herbs. Their trinkets of wood and stone, of twisted wire and twine. Their strangely accented tongue, and their tattoos, both permanent and painted on. Altogether, there was something otherworldly about them. Something that made his encounters with them feel as though they should be forbidden.

But Ydenia, it seemed, had found her people. The shamans nodded their heads when she asked about extending life. They were free with their secrets. And they welcomed her into their hovels and caves. For her part, she was free with giving them bits of her hair and even her blood for their spells. And she learned. Day by day she acquired knowledge that made her happy. And when she came back to the lean-to where they were making their bed at night, she shared her excitement with him.

Cedric was learning as well. The Gaidheal did not believe in writing anything down. And they wouldn't permit either Cedric or Ydenia to take notes while they were telling their tales. But their oral tradition was rich. They carried stories of the old gods Cedric had never heard before.

A few weeks into their visit, the shaman elders told Cedric and Ydenia about the gods' council, a time when all of the gods would gather together. But the idea of a trip north to the Krigsrike, where the councils were held, felt like a step backward. And the timing was wrong, regardless.

But the gods were one topic where Ydenia's studies and Cedric's overlapped. And when Ydenia learned that the gods could be summoned, Cedric anxiously agreed to participate in the rite that would call them forth. He was assured that it would require none of his blood or hair. And while he wasn't as devout as many of his peers, he was grateful to learn that it wouldn't require him to forswear his knight's oath to the One God.

On the night of the summoning, the shamans suggested that Cedric and Ydenia wear comfortable clothing. It might be a long ritual.

The head shaman guided Cedric and Ydenia to opposite sides of the fire. She bade them remain silent but keep in their thoughts any wishes they had for the evening's ceremony. She then ushered the other shamans to places between them. Altogether, including Cedric and Ydenia, there were eight people around the fire, and they formed a fairly regular circle.

Cedric watched as the head shaman left the circle and returned from the shadows with a wooden bowl containing a thick, milky liquid. She handed it to a shaman to the right of Ydenia. That shaman took a long quaff before passing the bowl slowly around the circle. Each participant took a healthy draught of the potion before passing it along, clockwise, to the next.

The head shaman disappeared again and returned with a bundle of sticks and herbs tied together with twine. She lit the bundle in the fire at the center of the ceremony. Once the bundle was burning well, she blew it out, and it began to issue forth smoke in gouts. She first bathed herself in the smoke, starting at her ankles and working her way up her own body. She then slowly paced around the circle, waving the pungent smoke at each participant with short strokes from a barred owl's feather. When she had cleansed everyone, she stepped from the circle again and set down the bundle, allowing the wind to carry away the smoke in a gentle upward spiral.

She watched the smoke briefly and appeared to meditate for a moment before she took her place in the circle, making them nine. She began to chant, and the others followed along with a low, rhythmic humming. Time passed. Cedric wasn't sure how long. But his thoughts wandered. He found himself following the embers rising as motes of light from the flames before him. Lit from below, and stark against the black backdrop of the surrounding forest, pieces of ash floated upward more slowly, like white and grey snowflakes. After a while, the light and shadow seemed to find a rhythm and a pattern that drew Cedric inward. Time slowed.

And then, suddenly, Mikele appeared beyond the flames. She was stunning. Auburn hair. Cream-white skin. And a dress that seemed grown of flowers and vines. Cedric sat up sharply, and Ydenia rose from her seat immediately, approached the goddess, and began to ask her questions. Mikele looked flattered by the attention. They sat down close by one another, and she quietly began to answer Ydenia's questions.

Cedric was trying to hear what they were saying, so he could recall it later for his notes, when another figure appeared. Mirren the Traveler materialized from the shadows beyond the fire. And he sat down at Cedric's side.

"You have questions?"

Cedric was nearly struck dumb. But the gaze of the old man before him was kind. And he found his voice.

"I want to know everything. About you, and the other gods. About your oldest memories. About your history—"

Mirren laughed. "We don't have time enough for that, I'm afraid. Well, I suppose *I* do. But you would be dead long before we got to any of the interesting parts."

Cedric pressed. "Then the beginning. Tell me about your origins."

Mirren smiled. And he began to talk.

7

MIRREN'S TALE

"My oldest memories are of dust. I remember living in a pall of it that seemed to go on forever. There were also dreams I had then, though not so much anymore. Strange dreams. Of another world. Perhaps another time.

"And my brother was there too. He was always there. Having each other made the dust bearable. We stumbled around together for . . . years, I suppose. Our minds seemed to work better after a while. And we began to think of things we could do to pass the time. I think I was the one who came up with the idea to find high ground—to see if we could get above the dust.

"I can't tell you how long we wandered. But we eventually found our way to the foot of a mountain. The climb was strange. I can

27

still remember that much. It was as if we were in the clouds. Only my brother and me, and nothing else around us but white and grey. At the summit, we discovered that my plan was a good one. We climbed up out of the dust onto the mountain's peak. It wasn't much more than a barren pile of rocks. But from our perch, we could see other mountains around us. Some were far taller than ours, and a few were green at the top. But we didn't dare climb down our mountain to seek these others out, because we were afraid we would never be able to keep our bearings to find our way to the next peak.

"That was when I learned that I could fly."

Cedric was in awe. He never would have imagined he could have this kind of access to one of the gods. And he didn't want to interrupt him. But ... "Tell me about that, please!"

Mirren's smile grew. "Well, as I was saying, we didn't dare leave our peak. In hindsight, I feel confident we would have been hopelessly turned around if we had. But one day ... I can't tell how many days we'd been up there, but one day, we spotted a massive bird. It was an albatross. The bird's name just came to me. It was the first creature my brother and I had seen beyond our dreams of what came before the dust. The albatross flew a long, arcing loop around our peak. But he must not have seen anything of interest, and he flew on toward one of the greener peaks. Many days passed after that before we saw another creature. There were times, much later, when I would look at Mirgul and say, 'Albatross?' And he would nod his head to reassure me that we had both seen the bird.

"On the day I learned I could fly, I was thinking of the albatross. I had closed my eyes. I was picturing the bird. And I tried to reach my mind outward, seeking the bird's spirit. Then I imagined *being* the bird. Soaring over the peaks. Floating above the dust. I felt myself lighten. When I opened my eyes, I was floating. Somehow it didn't shock me. Mirgul applauded! And he tried to float as well.

"Days later, so many anxious days later, he finally got the hang of it. By then I had moved beyond simply floating and, with some practice, had discovered that I could assume the form of an albatross. As the albatross, I would fly in circles about our mountain. I desperately wanted to soar across to the other peaks. To explore. To see if there were other creatures out there. But I didn't want to leave my brother behind. He was sensitive enough about not being able to fly.

That would have made him even more solemn.

"On the day he learned to float, I took him by the hand, and we left our mountain. I'd say for good, except that we sometimes went back there, as the dust sank lower and lower with time. We would look at what the dust was revealing as it settled."

When Mirren paused, Cedric couldn't help himself. "Where did you go, then, and what did you see?"

"We found . . . *life!*" His smile was enormous. "That was what I like to think of as the true beginning of things. There were plants and trees, birds and animals. Some of these things were as they had been in our dreams. Some were different. Some had changed in subtle ways. Some seemed to be creatures sprung anew from a dream—or a nightmare. And we found Mikele!" He glanced over at the goddess, who looked up at her name, and he won a warm smile from her.

He continued. "Over the centuries, we found other gods. Maybe as many as fifty. Maybe more. There were also humans and elves. Dwarves and giants. Gnomes. Kobolds. Dragons. Most of these creatures couldn't fly, and none but the gods could change their form. And these others, these living beings, needed food and shelter. When they realized that we did not, and when the more martial among them attacked us and realized they couldn't harm us in any way, some of them took to worshipping us."

Mirren paused. And Cedric's mind felt as though it were expanding inside his skull. But the god continued. "Is this what you came for? Is this what you sought?"

Cedric nodded. "It's more than I ever imagined I would experience, to hear you describe it all. I am quite stunned by all of this. I would sit down with you sometime and try to write it all down—and whatever other lore you might be willing to share."

Mirren smiled. "Of course. I have all the time in the world. You can have as much of it as you want. Just don't squander the little time you have, as a mortal, and waste it talking to me."

The god shared more with Cedric, though many of the rest of his words were lost to him, because Cedric must have fallen asleep while the god spoke. He awoke beside the cooling embers of the fire to discover Ydenia by his side. And both the gods were gone.

He sat up. And he fumbled for the pack containing his journal. He would need to write everything down while it was still fresh. And then he cursed. *He had never thought to ask Mirren about his falling-out with Mirgul!*

8

MAGIC AND PINE NUTS

A few days had passed since their evening with Mirren and Mikele, and Ydenia came back to their lean-to very late one evening. Cedric was rubbing an unguent into his bad leg as best he could, considering the awkward angles involved, when she entered.

"Oh, good! Your leg is bare. I want to try something."

Cedric frowned at her. "Are you sure of what you're about? No experiments on your ... on *me* lest you're sure you won't cause more harm than good!" He'd been about to say, what . . . lover? Partner? Helpmeet? Friend? But in her eagerness, she didn't seem to notice the hitch in his words.

"Of course you can trust me! Turn over onto your stomach."

Cedric grudgingly did as she ordered.

She placed both hands on his withered calf. And she gently moved each hand in counterrotating circles on either side of his leg. He felt nothing at first. Then he felt a warming sensation. She was moving too slowly for the heat to be coming from the friction of the motion itself. Then there was a *wiggling* in the center of his muscle. It suddenly tickled so badly he couldn't restrain himself from bucking his hips. But she was able to continue uninterrupted until the next *squirm* in his muscle caused him to buck even harder. This time, she lost her balance and tumbled backward, nearly out of their shelter.

She was angry as she rose to continue. "Stop that and let me work!"

But Cedric was already turning over and sitting up.

"No. I've had enough magic for tonight. Perhaps tomorrow. I am tired. And I was not prepared for this . . . whatever *that* was."

She persisted. "Come now. I was working the spell as she taught me. You didn't give me a chance—"

"I'm sorry. I'm tired. And again, I think I need to prepare myself mentally if you are going to try that again."

She acquiesced—grudgingly. But when

she finally climbed under the blankets, she faced away from him and offered him her back.

As Cedric tried to fall asleep that night, he considered the moment earlier, when he hadn't known how to categorize the relationship he had with Ydenia. Before they had left Ekszer Hegy, they had sometimes shared a bed. And it had become routine on their travels these past months. They spent any time not among their books and research in each other's company. But they had never talked of marrying or living a life together beyond their studies.

The rational part of him could acknowledge that they were not a perfect match. Her temper was short. She did not have a great deal of patience for his mannerisms—like his idle humming while he read, or his newfound habit of praying before he ate and slept. She was dismissive of his growing faith in the One God in general, in fact. And she thought he cared too much about finding the right and wrong in everyday situations.

For his part, he had to confess to himself that the luster of what he had once thought of as her refreshing spontaneity now felt more like a lingering fear of whatever outburst might come next. She gave him something though. A spark. Feelings of passion that gave his life a vibrancy in her presence. Emotions he had never experienced with other women. His books and his studies had always seemed enough to fill his life. But Ydenia regularly challenged him to be more than his studies—by her words but also by her mere existence, and the example she set for him in the way she lived her life.

Still, he realized that the likelihood of them staying together was not high. How long would they pretend that they had a future together? Would he be the one to broach the topic? Or, more likely, would she do so on a night like tonight, in a moment of anger?

He lay awake for some time before sleep claimed him and quieted his thoughts.

THE NEXT MORNING, Cedric awoke to the smell of pine nuts roasting on their campfire. Ydenia must have risen much earlier to have collected them, started the fire, and gotten them toasting. She wasted no further time when she noticed he was awake.

"I want to work on your leg again."

Cedric had almost forgotten about her ministrations the night before. Unconsciously he reached down and squeezed his calf to work out some of its perpetual tightness, which had never gone away these past thirty years. The muscle wasn't as tight as he had expected it to be. He flexed his foot up and down. It wasn't much of a difference. But he thought perhaps . . .

"Okay. I'll let you work on it again. But you might need to get some Gaidheal to sit on me while you work. I don't think I'll be able to keep myself from bucking you off again if it feels the same as it did last night!"

She smiled. Everything was so much better when she smiled.

He continued. "And I'm hungry. Famished, actually. Do we have anything more than these pine nuts?"

She frowned. "I was up early collecting them, and all you can do is complain they won't be enough? We have no food. And these people don't take money. How long has it been since we sold our horses, and how far did that even get us? I've run out of things to trade with them. We need to find some other type of barter. I don't want to starve out here just because they won't take our coin!"

Cedric shared her frown. "We ate all the dried mushrooms, didn't we? I suppose I could hunt—"

"Hunt? Among the Gaidheal, who eat no meat! How do you think they would feel about that?"

Cedric grunted. He supposed she was probably right.

"I've some things I could trade that aren't coin. There's the silver ore . . ."

She shook her head. "They have enough precious metal here. And they don't value it the same way we do. Besides, I know that hunk of metal has special meaning to you. Or you wouldn't still have it after all these years. I'll go to the village, and I'll see what I can do. I will collect some things and bring them with me to see if I can make a trade of some kind."

She grabbed her pack and she was off. Just like that, without even eating any of the breakfast she'd so painstakingly collected and prepared. He forced himself to get up and take their breakfast off the fire. It would be a crime to let the pine nuts burn.

9

RESTORATION

The pages of *The Prophecy of Usen* were getting harder to read as dusk settled in. Ydenia had not yet returned. Cedric had found some eggs in the woods and had them for lunch. He had collected a handful of mushrooms as well. Those he had saved, despite a growling stomach, against Ydenia's return—in case she had not had any luck.

But when she came back, she wore a broad smile and had a sack full of food. Three loaves of a dense bread, a hard hunk of sheep cheese, and a handful of apples. Enough food for a few days if they rationed it carefully.

"Well done! I also found some more mushrooms."

"Well, let's eat, then! I want to get to working on that leg of yours."

Cedric laughed. "You are relentless!"

That smile again. He felt a small shiver run down his neck and shoulders. Their life was simple. But moments like these made him feel it was hard to imagine wanting anything more from it.

"Some bread and a little cheese now, then. And maybe we can put the mushrooms and cheese on a piece of bread later and heat it in the fire."

His mouth watered at her words. "I'll tell you what, let's make that cheese and mushroom toast of yours now. When I've had my fill, you can work your magic on my leg. And I won't resist, though I can't promise I won't buck again."

She faked a frown at not getting her way. "Fine. We eat a good meal now, and then I get back to your leg. But I've thought of a way to work on your leg where I won't be in as much danger. I'll hold your legs in my lap and work on it from below."

Cedric considered. "That might prove easier."

In no time at all, Ydenia had used elemental magic to restore the fire. The bread was cut, the mushrooms roasted, and the cheese and mushrooms melted together on top of four thick slabs of toast. Cedric broke out a pouch of salt from his bag and sprinkled some on top for good measure. Then he took a bite. *Amazing!* All the flavors came together in his mouth to create a taste of something entirely new.

"Wow. This is much better than I expected."

She nodded her head. Her mouth was full. And before she finished swallowing, "Delishush!"

CEDRIC HADN'T FELT SO satisfied from a meal in some time. And he happily complied with Ydenia's attentions after they'd put away the uneaten bread and cheese.

She had piled up their packs not too far from the fire, and she propped her back up against them. Then she had Cedric lie on his back, with his legs on her lap. His left side, with the bad leg, was facing the fire. After they had both shifted their positions a few times to get comfortable, she wasted no time in once again placing her hands on his leg.

The squirming and wiggling sensation came back quickly. But he was able to resist the urge to flinch. As she kept at it, the squirming grew and expanded within his calf. Soon his entire calf felt as though it were filled with snakes, shifting and wriggling within his muscles. There were a few brief spikes of pain. But it was the wriggling sensation that was most disconcerting. It would be hard to imagine letting anyone else do this to him. But he felt he owed it to Ydenia to let her try. And if by some miracle she could heal his leg after all these years . . .

He watched her face as she concentrated. She was in her element. This was what she was meant to be and meant to do. He smiled even as he fought to resist the urge to kick out with his leg.

After what seemed an eternity but was probably half an hour, she slowed her hand movements, stopped them, and rested her hands against his leg. She looked drawn. *She must be exhausted!*

And his leg . . . his leg felt *very* different. Something had definitely changed. But he wanted to be sure before he let himself get too excited. He carefully extracted himself from her lap, gave his calf a quick squeeze to test it out, and then stood. His calf was healed. Entirely. After all these years. As if he had never been bitten by that troll. He didn't understand. *How was that possible?*

10

FORAGING

Over the next few weeks, Cedric hardly saw Ydenia. She was either meeting with the shamans, looking for sick people and animals to practice on, or back in the village, bartering. He often didn't see her until very late at night.

So Cedric had taken to walking the woods. His new leg made him feel young again and, as much as he almost despised the words he was thinking, since they seemed the words of a brash young soldier more than a respected old scholar, *more of a man again*. As such, he wanted to do his part to contribute to their subsistence. Midsummer would arrive in a few days. While many, like the Krigares, thought that was a reason to celebrate, Cedric also knew that it meant the turning point. The day after which the nights grew longer. And he wanted to make sure they were prepared to weather the cold—if they were going to spend the winter among the Gaidheal.

He had strayed farther each day and taken to carrying a large, open, sling-like bag for collecting. He was having fair success collecting edible plants—leaves and tubers, which he had been stockpiling, and even some early fruit, some of which he had also been stockpiling. He would occasionally stumble on mushrooms and eggs. And he was now having no trouble supplying the food they needed.

He had found a brook in the forest. And after a morning of quiet watching, he'd spotted some trout in it. He was indulging himself by building a fish trap in the shallows upstream from a deep pool. He was plunging sticks into the riverbed in the form of a V, and then creating a pen at the narrow end of the V to contain the fish that managed to navigate in through the funnel. He heard a twig snap and looked up to see a small elf girl, with a tangle of wavy hair the color of strawberries. If she had been human, he'd have guessed she was no more than ten years old. But he knew that elves aged more slowly.

"What are you doing?" Her voice was

high, as one might expect from a girl her age. But she spoke to him boldly.

He smiled at her warmly. "I plan to catch some fish."

She stepped closer and frowned. "I don't understand."

"You see, the fish will swim into this wide opening here. And they will find their way through the narrow hole here. But once they have passed through, they will have a hard time finding it again to escape, because it is so narrow from the other side."

"Will that really work? I don't see why they won't find their way out again."

Cedric shrugged, causing his rolled-up pant leg to fall into the water. He laughed. "The book I read on woodcraft tells me it will, though I must confess I've never constructed one before."

The girl looked up at something over Cedric's shoulder, and he turned around. On the bank behind him was a slender young . . . *elf*. Or more likely a half-elf, if he were any judge. He wore a large knife at his belt and had a long bow over his shoulder and across his chest. But his hands were empty. And while his gaze was flat, he didn't appear to be threatening.

"Oh . . . hullo! My name is Cedric. Is this little one your charge, then?"

The half-elf allowed the question to hang in the air a moment longer than most people would before responding. "She is."

"Very good." Cedric wondered what he might say to convince the man that he was no threat to the girl.

And then the young man spoke again. "It will work. You've chosen a good spot for it, though you will want to close those wider gaps in your pen, of course."

It took Cedric a moment to realize that he was talking about the fish trap. Once he did, he beamed, suddenly delighted. "You think? Oh, that's wonderful. Thank you! Do you have experience with these traps, then?"

The half-elf merely nodded this time. Then he addressed the girl. "Come, sister. We should be getting you back. Our mother expects you in Aoilfhionn in two days' time. Best we not dally any longer than we already have." He turned to Cedric and nodded again. "Good fishing." Then he loped off to the north, and the little elf girl followed behind him, easily keeping up with his long-legged pace.

She didn't say anything as they moved away, but she glanced over her shoulder twice. Once to give a final glance to Cedric's trap, and a second time to meet his eyes before she turned her head forward and disappeared into the trees after her brother.

Cedric sighed and drew a deep breath. He'd probably been breathing shallowly the whole time. He relaxed his shoulders. They were tight.

He retrieved more sticks from the pile he had built on the edge of the brook. With a few more minutes' attention, he finished his trap. And he now had reason to believe it might actually work. *What a serendipitous encounter!* He climbed out of the brook one last time and wrung out his sopping pant leg as best he could. Then he began the long walk back to camp, a new spring in his step.

11

SUBTERFUGE

When Cedric returned to camp, he noticed that his pack had been disturbed. It was sitting the way he always left it, but the flap wasn't tucked in the way he liked it to be. He rummaged through it to see if anything was missing. His journal was in its usual pouch, but it was upside down. Everything else appeared to be untouched. His journal? Who could possibly have any interest in his journal? It surely wasn't Ydenia. She could have simply asked him what he was writing.

He considered what he'd been writing about. Gnome activity was reportedly on the rise. And the Gaidheal seemed to think that it was the Laonese pushing their borders again. He'd draft a letter stating as much to the king if he encountered anyone traveling that way.

But in the meantime, his notes would have to serve to collect his intelligence. That said, there was nothing damning in his writing. Not even for Laon. At worst, he was a gadfly, buzzing about the lands and giving his king a reason to justify letting him pursue his studies. *Who*, then?

As long as the day was, it was beginning to grow short. And the light would start to fail soon. As if to prove something to his trespasser, Cedric grabbed his journal and a vial of ink and prepared a quill to write. He would document the work he had done today to build the fish trap, and describe the elves he had encountered. Let them make something of *that*!

Ydenia arrived before the dark was complete. Cedric had a fire burning. And he was trying to guess at who might be interested in his journals when she returned. She looked . . . *determined*. Not an unusual aspect of hers. But tonight she seemed especially intense.

"What is it?" He knew she wouldn't be likely to keep him in suspense. But her appearance was concerning.

She focused her gaze on him. "I am facing a difficulty."

He almost smiled. It was so rare for her ever to admit to weakness. But she was too serious for him to make a joke.

"Go on."

"Those weeks ago, when we ran out of food . . . I bartered for bread and cheese that one day. And I was able to trickle in other food over the days following."

Cedric's mind began jumping from one fearful conclusion to another. He even recalled that she'd never volunteered precisely *what* she'd had to trade for that food. But he held his tongue.

"My barter was to report on you. To a man I met at the market. By his accent, I assumed he was from Laon. By now I've realized that he is a Laonese agent, though he never said as much outright."

Cedric allowed himself to breathe again. He'd already been contemplating the fact that he had nothing to hide. "Ydenia . . . it's okay. I hardly represent a threat to his nation."

But Ydenia shook her head. "I lied to him. I told him you were a spy who worked for the Hyrden king."

Cedric cocked his head somewhat to one side. "Well, I suppose on some level that is true—"

"But I made things up. When I told him

the truth, he hardly seemed interested. He told me such matters weren't worthy of barter. So I told him more. And more. Until I was sure he was taking me seriously. And he would be willing to pay for what I could offer."

Cedric waited. He wasn't about to chastise *Ydenia*. Not for something she was in the middle of confessing. Not when he knew that doing so would give her the opportunity to turn her disappointment in herself into anger at *him*.

She continued. "I think we are in danger. Well . . . I am certain *you* are."

Cedric chose his next words carefully. "What do you think we should do about all of this?"

She shook her head. "I'm not sure. I've only ever dealt with the one man. But when I met with him this afternoon, he mentioned that he was meeting up with some associates tonight."

Cedric had never heard anxiety in Ydenia's tone before. And she still hadn't technically apologized. But at least she was telling the truth of what she had done.

"Does he know where our camp is? Do you think we should leave?"

She nodded. "He does. I had to make sure you wouldn't surprise him by coming back to our camp while he was looking through your journal. So I stood watch."

For the first time, the full weight of what had been done to him sank in. He felt violated. That she should allow a stranger to go through his things? To read his journal? Part of him knew he'd have a hard time handling that particular notebook again and continuing his diary as if nothing had happened.

He was contemplating how to tell her what her actions meant to him. As it was, he wasn't yet sure what her betrayal would mean for their relationship. But he didn't want to summon words too quickly that might put even more distance between them.

And then he noticed a group of men moving quickly down the path toward their camp.

"Ydenia! Watch yourself!"

She turned, startled. And he watched her visage transform from sadness to rage in a moment.

Okay. She was prepared. Or at least aware. Now, what were the two of them going to do against three men armed with swords and clubs?

Damn it! Why didn't he still carry his sword? He had left his arms and armor behind when he left for Ekszer Hegy, presuming he'd never have need of them again, due to his injury. He looked around for something to wield. His walking stick. He hadn't even carved it. It was simply a found stick, of just the right length, that a beaver had left behind for him to find. It would have to serve. He bolted for it, covering the distance quickly.

He was reaching for the stick when a club came down on the back of his head. His vision narrowed, like black curtains drawn closed across his sight from either side.

12

JUSTICE

Cedric awoke with a start. Ydenia's face hovered upside down over his own. She was gripping the sides of his head firmly with both hands. He relaxed his guard. But his body still felt tense. Or . . . alert? He started to sit up and Ydenia didn't resist. She allowed her hands to slump into her lap. As he rose from the ground, he remembered that he had been knocked out. There must have been a fourth man, who'd snuck up behind him. Cedric had been hit on the head before he'd even had a chance to swing his walking stick. He reached up to feel for a lump. Nothing. For that matter, he felt exceptionally well. Not just well. Not just healed. But renewed. Ydenia must have worked magic on him again.

And then he smelled overcooked meat.

He looked around for the source. But their campfire was nothing more than ash. "Ydenia . . . are you okay?" She looked exhausted. He stood up fully to look around—for a threat from the Laonese who had jumped him. Then he saw the first body—charred beyond his ability to tell more than the fact that the corpse had been humanlike. A head. Two arms. Two legs. All burned black as coal. A quick look around revealed two more bodies, equally incinerated.

He scowled and looked down at Ydenia, realizing at once what the fire magic would have cost her, and knowing that her study of healing had granted her an affinity for perceiving the pain of others. She was half sitting, half kneeling, and her head was bowed almost to the ground.

"Ydenia . . ."

Nothing.

He took a knee and crouched down close to her. Even in this difficult moment, he found himself acknowledging that his joints didn't creak or complain as he did so.

"Ydenia . . ." He gently cupped her chin in his hand and raised her face to his own. Her eyes were vacant. No, not quite vacant. There was something there he thought might be regret. What he wouldn't give to see a bit of her feisty nature right now.

A twig broke behind him, and Cedric stood and spun on his heels in a single fluid motion, like a man half his age. Even as he saw the man in a huntsman's concealing garb of brown and green, poised to kill him, Cedric registered something that had been nagging at him. *The fourth man!* The one who'd snuck up on him before! There were only three bodies!

Likely because his opponent hadn't expected the speed and agility of Cedric's maneuver, the man's sword thrust narrowly missed him. Better yet, the sword stuck in the ground behind Cedric, and he was able to strike downward on the man's overextended arm and knock the man's hand free from the weapon's hilt. The man started to reach for his dagger, and Cedric instinctively wrapped his arms around his attacker, pinning the man's arms to his sides and tackling him to the ground. Cedric felt so hale and hearty right now that he thought he would be able to bring down a platoon of Laonese soldiers.

But what now? If he killed the man, he couldn't learn what he'd been up to. But if he didn't, would he be able to subdue him? The strength he felt course through his body convinced him to try.

He let go of the man with one hand and punched him in the face. The man's nose crunched satisfactorily. That would help his chances. He knew that fighting with a broken nose made it harder to see and much harder to focus on what you were doing. Instinctively the man's now free left arm came up to his face to protect it from further assault. Cedric leaned his weight on the man and tried to shift his own body enough that he could remove the man's dagger from his belt without releasing his other arm. It was easier than he had expected. And once he had the dagger in hand, he held it to the man's throat.

"I will slit your throat right now if you don't stop thrashing about!"

The other man stopped trying to rock his body out from underneath Cedric.

"Better. Now, tell me what you and your comrades here were up to?"

The man spat a gob of spit and blood into Cedric's face.

"So much for diplomacy." Cedric struck the man on the side of the head with the pommel of the dagger as hard as he could. He felt something give as he followed through with the blow. And he realized too late that he'd probably used too much force. *Oh well. He was certainly ready to do me in without any remorse.*

But whether the man would ultimately survive the injury or not, he was now unconscious and breathing shallowly. Cedric assumed he was not much more of a threat. That said, he was prudent enough to quickly cut away the man's outer coat and make rough strips out of it to bind his hands behind him. He left him there, on his side in the leaves, and he rose to go back and check on Ydenia.

But his revitalized strength and stamina failed him when he took in the sight before him. Ydenia was still half kneeling, half sitting on the forest floor. But the soldier's sword was buried in her chest.

13

STARTING OVER

After he had given Ydenia a primitive burial in the woods by their camp, Cedric left for Arlon the next day. The man he had struck in the head didn't survive. He had been dead when Cedric had woken up that morning. And there was nothing on his person to give Cedric a clue about his activities. No missives. Only some coin and food, and his sword and dagger. Cedric took all of it —and the man's belt and scabbard as well.

Despite some misgivings, Cedric also decided to leave him unburied. The three charred bodies, he also left where they lay. Let anyone who came along wonder at who the bodies had been. Perhaps they might think it was Cedric and Ydenia. He didn't care. He just knew that his heart was heavy.

And he wanted to leave Shenn Frith, and all of its memories, behind him.

ON HIS WAY, he stopped to check on his fish trap. Two fat brook trout were swimming in tight circles in the pen he'd constructed. He went to remove his harvesting sack from his pack, then changed his mind. Instead, he used his walking stick to pry apart enough of the sticks to create a wider opening in the pen. The smaller fish was out in a flash and disappeared back into the deeper waters downstream. Cedric waited to see that the larger fish found its way out as well. It didn't take long.

Cedric looked at the forest around him. The beauty of his surroundings caused an ache in his chest. The morning sunlight dappling through the trees. The purling of the brook at his feet. The warm smells of loam, and the sharp, bright scent of pine. He knew it was one of those moments that came along fairly regularly if you spent enough time in the woods. And he almost expected a rabbit, fox, or deer to appear and complete the picture.

It seemed so obvious to Cedric that such beauty could only be a gift. There must be a benevolent creator behind it all. How else could one explain it?

He'd read so many writings about religion and the gods. And he'd even met two of them. But despite all his studies, or perhaps, even more accurately, *because of* them, he knew in his heart that Mirren and Mikele hadn't created the world around him. Mirren himself had even said as much—albeit indirectly.

So who, then? It could only be the One God of Usen's prophecy. Or, if not Him, then a being equally as great and powerful. The thought, as ever, was a humbling one.

He readjusted his pack, and although he knew better, he glanced in the direction the elves had gone, as if he expected to see them there again. They were probably most of the way back to Aoilfhionn by now.

Cedric contemplated his next steps. Arlon seemed the most logical place for him to go. Now that his leg was healed, perhaps his king would even grant him a position in the army again. At his age, and with his education, he liked to think he'd make a fine knight-captain. Ydenia's gift of a renewed body even had him envisaging holding a sword again.

In any event, he'd have ample time to consider his prospects on the long walk back to the capital.

14

ABSOLUTION

Nearly five years had passed since Cedric had said goodbye to Ydenia in the forest of Shenn Frith. He thought of her often. When he was standing before a mirror, and the face of a man much younger than his years looked back at him, he thought about her magic. How she had somehow done more than just heal him. She had restored much of his youth and vitality as well. When he thought about the ongoing conflict with Laon, and her ill-advised attempt to fleece Laonese spies out of what amounted to a petty sum of money—ultimately at the cost of her life. When he considered the very meaning of his own existence, and whether he would ever meet a woman with whom he might choose to share his life.

Ydenia had not been a perfect woman. He

smiled. *Whatever that might mean.* But she'd had more spirit than anyone else he had ever known. Her pride had ultimately been her undoing. And perhaps a slip in integrity. Such a small slip, with such enormous consequences.

He turned to the last entry in his current journal and read the words he had written the night before.

Journal of Cedric Warke, Year 884 of the One God
    Arlon—Day 223

After five more years of military service, some served as knight-general during the Laonese Rebellion, the king has granted me a release. Putting down the plots and treachery of Laon, and others, has sapped my spirit. And my conscience is heavy with thoughts of the blood I've spilled on behalf of Hyrde. But my king is gracious and is allowing me to leave his service and take up the cloth.

Truth be told, I think my piety since I came back has worn thin for him. He is probably just as glad to see my moralizing go with me. Becoming a priest was nothing I had ever thought I'd do with my life. But I've lived longer than a normal man should. It seems only right to dedi-

cate my remaining years to the service of the One God. He saw me through the darkest moments of my days. I see now that He was always there. Even when I forgot about Him or strayed from His teachings.

In any event, I will be able to resume my studies—this time with more of a focus on enhancing my faith—at the monastery at Ridderzaal. He asked only one boon of me in the bargain: to make good use of all my studies these many years and teach whatever youth of the kingdom might be in need of an education. Being a perennial student myself, I could hardly say no. It is only through the generosity, patience, and goodwill of those who have taught me over these many years that I am the man I am today.

CEDRIC PLACED the last of his journals in the crate. He'd lived nearly a lifetime at the service of his king. And he would finally be free of the plots and machinations of court. He walked out of his study and informed his aide that the last few items were ready to be loaded onto the wagon.

EPILOGUE

A covered walkway extended from the western face of the monastery to a postern gate at the left rear corner of Ridderzaal Castle. To the left of a large double-doored entrance on the northeastern face of the monastery was a small footpath that led to one of the outbuildings and a much smaller door.

Cedric ran his fingers over the coarse wool of his undyed robe. No more uniforms. No more politics. But would he ever get used to the scratch of this cassock?

He reached the door and grasped the large iron ring, knocking firmly three times.

The wait felt long, but within about a minute, Cedric detected footsteps beyond the door, and shortly thereafter it opened, revealing a middle-aged cleric in a robe just like his own.

"Oh, good! Brother Cedric, is it? You've come at an auspicious time. We've just taken on a handful of young students we have agreed to teach. Four nobles and a crafts-man's son . . ."

ALSO BY MATTHEW B. BERG

Available Now!

A Monk's Tale - The first novelette released in the world of The Crafter Chronicles

The Crafter's Son - Book One of the Exciting New Coming of Age Epic Fantasy Series, The Crafter Chronicles

Coming Soon (in 2020)!

The Queen & The Soldier - Book Two of the Exciting New Coming of Age Epic Fantasy Series, The Crafter Chronicles

The Orphan's Plight (working title) - Another novelette in the world of The Crafter Chronicles

Coming in 2021 . . .

The Ranger King - Book Three of the Exciting New Coming of Age Epic Fantasy Series, The Crafter Chronicles

The Lay of Legorel (working title) - Yet another novelette in the world of The Crafter Chronicles

A BRIEF GLOSSARY, WITH
PRONUNCIATIONS

Aelric - *(ALE-Rick) - A half-elf ranger.*
Aoilfhionn - *(Ā-ō-lən) - The city of trees. Capital city of Fardach Sidhe, homeland of the elves.*
Arlon - *(ar-LON) - The capital of Hyrde, and seat of the kingdom.*
Ath - *(rhymes with bath) - A land comprised of mountains and a fertile river valley. Home of the giants. It occupies the northeast region of Erda.*
bailey - *(BĀ-lē) - A defensive wall that encloses the land surrounding a castle. Also can*

refer to the area enclosed by
such a wall.

Beltide - *(BEL-tide)* - A holiday
celebrating the arrival of
spring.

Bertil - *(BURR-til)* - A dwarven
smith of ancient legend.

Birghid - *(burr-3ĒD)* - Goddess
of wisdom and beauty.

Culuden - *(CƏ-lə-den)* - Capital
city of Pretania. Seat of the
Pretanian clan chief.

Dvargheim - *(DVARG-hīm)* -
Mountainous home of the
dwarves, occupying the
eastern region of Erda.

Ekszer Hegy - *(ECK-Zurr HEH-
gee)* - An island off the
dwarven coast of Dvargheim.
Home to a fortress run by
wizards and scholars.

Erda - *(UR-dä)* - The continent of
known lands where The
Crafter's Son *takes place.*

Fardach Sidhe - *(far-däk SHĒ)* -
Forested homeland of the
Elves, occupying the western
region of Erda.

Gaidheal - *(GĀ-ell)* - The ancient
name of the people of the land

of Shenn Frith, who are
colloquially referred to as
Shenn Frith.

Geornlice - *(JORN-liss)* -
Southern land known for its
swamps and bayous.
Inhabited predominantly by
gnomes.

Götar - *(GÖ-tär)* - Dwarf god
of war.

Hyrde - *(HĒRD)* - Central region
of Erda. Homeland of Cedric.

Hyrden - *(HĒRDen)* - The people
of Hyrde.

Jetningen - *(JET-ning-en)* -
Mountainous land to the east
of Erda. Inhabited by trolls.

Krigare - *(CREE-gar)* - The war-
like race of people living in
the north.

Krigsrike - *(KRĒG's-rike)* - Home
of the Krigare. The land
occupying the northern-most
region of Erda.

Laon - *(LAY-on)* - The
breadbasket of Erda. A flat
land of rich soil where a
majority of the grain
consumed in Erda is
produced. Occupying the

southwest corner of Erda,
between the forests of
Fardach Sidhe and Shenn
Frith, and the swamplands of
Geornlice.

Laonese - *(LAY-on-ēz) - The
people of Laon.*

Long Lake - *A large lake which
forms the eastern border of
Hyrde. To the east of the lake
lie Jetningen and Dvargheim.*

Mahjar - *(MÄ-ʒar) - A tribal and
nomadic race of humans from
the Namur region, famed for
their horses. All Mahjars are
from Namur. But not all
people of Namur are of the
race of the Mahjar.*

Mikele - *(mi-KEL-lay) - A
goddess and patron/protector
of the Gaidheal.*

Miremont - *(MIR-ə-mont) - A
large trade city in central
Laon.*

Mirgul - *(MEER-gül) - A god.
Brother to Mirren.*

Mirren - *(MIR-en) - A god.
Brother to Mirgul.*

Mungo - *(Mung-go) - Pretani god
of luck.*

Namur - *(NÄ-mur) - A land of rolling hills and wild grassland where the Namur people raise their herds of half-tame horses. It occupies the region between Pretania to the west, Krigsrike to the north, Ath to the east, and Hyrde to the south.*

Pretania - *(pre-TÄN-ya) - A land of high elevation with a challenging terrain composed of bluffs and steep hills, occupying the northwest region of Erda.*

Pretani/Pretanian - *(pre-TÄN-ē/pre-TÄN-ē-ǝn) - The people of Pretania.*

Raulin - *(Raw-lin) - The King of Hyrde, Laon, and Pretania.*

Rhonwen - *(RON-wen) - An elven princess and warrior.*

Ridderzaal *(RID-ur-zäl) - The name of the castle, and the city which surrounds it, in the south of Hyrde, on Long Lake.*

Shenn Frith - *(shenn FRITH) - A small region of land located in the western forests of Erda,*

occupied by the Gaidheal.
Also, the name commonly
used to describe the people of
that land.

Usen - *(YÜ-sen)* - Prophet of the
One God.

Ydenia - *(ē-DĒN-yə)* - A
journeyman mage, and friend
of Cedric.

* *Stress/emphasis is shown by
word parts in ALL CAPS
(non-stressed syllables are in
lower case). Where I've used
symbols or diacritical marks,
here is what they mean!*

a - *"a" as in* bad
ä- *"ah" as in* ma *or* father
ā - *"ay" as in* day
ə - *"uh" as in* duh *or* what
e - *"e" as in* bed
ē- *"ee" as in* feed
i - *"ih" as in* dip
ī– *"ii" as in* wide
ʒ - *"zh" as in* version *or* usual
ö - *"oe" as in* voyeur
ō- *"oh" as in* go
ü- *"oo" as in* goose *or* blue

A Brief Glossary, with pronunciations

Other:

Knight-Captain - *A commanding
officer of an army of knights
and accompanying foot
soldiers.*

Knight-General - *A commanding
officer in charge of a nation's
army in times of war.*

Currency:
1 gold crown = 10 silver swans
*1 silver swan = 10 copper
commons*

Join the Crafter's Guild!

This book may have ended. But your journey begins now.

Join the guild and become part of the story.

- Members of the guild are always the first to hear about Matthew's new books and publications.
- Members will receive access to free behind-the-scenes content, such as maps, character sheets, and other Crafter artifacts—as we create them.
- Finally, some lucky guild members will have the opportunity to become beta readers for book two (and beyond!).

Join the Crafter's Guild!
http://www.matthewbberg.com/join

Reviews needed!

Like the book? If so, it would mean a lot to me if you would leave a review on Amazon or Goodreads.

Many people won't gamble on a new writer. So the more positive reviews I can accumulate, the more likely it is for other readers to give my work a chance.

Thanks in advance for your help!

ABOUT THE AUTHOR

Matthew Berg is a Director of IT by day, a dad and husband by night and weekend, and a writer by commute. He loves to travel—though mostly for the food. He's been playing D&D (on and off) since he and his brothers picked up the *Basic Set* at Lauriat's Books in 1977. He is known to attend renaissance fairs in period garb. And he has far, far too many hobbies.

Since his first book was released only two months before the writing of this story, he doesn't have compelling quotes about his work to share from authors like Terry Brooks and Brandon Sanderson. Yet. But when he does, you can be sure he'll include them here in his author's biography.

Made in the USA
Columbia, SC
30 March 2020